All of Our Noses Are Here

An I Can Read Book®

All of Our Noses Are Here

and Other Noodle Tales

Retold by Alvin Schwartz

Pictures by Karen Ann Weinhaus

HarperCollins*Publishers*

ALL OF OUR NOSES ARE HERE AND OTHER NOODLE TALES
Text copyright © 1985 by Alvin Schwartz
Illustrations copyright © 1985 by Karen Ann Weinhaus
All rights reserved. No part of this book may be
used or reproduced in any manner whatsoever without
written permission except in the case of brief quotations
embodied in critical articles and reviews. Printed in
the United States of America. For information address
HarperCollins Children's Books, a division of HarperCollins
Publishers, 10 East 53rd Street, New York, NY 10022.
Designed by Trish Parcell
10   9   8   7   6   5   4

Library of Congress Cataloging-in-Publication Data
Schwartz, Alvin, date
    All of our noses are here, and other noodle tales.

    (An I can read book)
    Summary: A collection of five stories about a
family of silly people, based on noodle folklore
from America, India, Japan, Korea, and the Arabian
Nights.
    1. Tales. [1. Folklore. 2. Humorous stories]
I. Weinhaus, Karen Ann, ill. II. Title. III. Series.
PZ7.S4A 1985   [E] [398.2]   84-48330
ISBN 0-06-025287-1
ISBN 0-06-025288-X (lib. bdg.)

Contents

Foreword

Most noodles

are kind and loving people.

But they have very few brains.

This book is about

a whole family of noodles

and the silly things they do.

They are Mr. and Mrs. Brown,
and their children Sam and Jane,
and Grandpa.

1. Jane Gets a Donkey

Mr. and Mrs. Brown

gave Jane a donkey

for her birthday.

She named him Jim.

That very day she and Sam

took Jim for a long ride.

9

On the way home

they stopped to buy some apples.

They left Jim

tied to a parking meter.

But while they were gone,

two men decided to steal him.

"I have a plan,"

said the leader.

"You take the donkey to the market

and sell him.

I will take care of things here."

10

The leader

put on Jim's halter

and tied himself

to the parking meter.

When Sam and Jane came back,

they were very surprised.

"Where is my donkey?" asked Jane.

"I am your donkey," said the thief.

"My father is a magician.

When I did not obey him,

he turned me into a donkey.

Now he has forgiven me.

He has turned me back

into a human.

Please let me go home."

"Of course," said Jane.

She took off the halter

and set him free.

"I hope you will be happy,"

she said.

Then she and Sam walked home.

The next day

Mr. Brown went to the market

with Sam and Jane

to buy another donkey.

There they saw Jim.

He was for sale again.

"Oh, no!" cried Jane.

"They have had another quarrel.

His father has turned him

into a donkey again!"

2. Grandpa Misses the Boat

Grandpa took the ferryboat
across the river to visit his friend.
But he was having such a good time,
he missed the last boat home.

18

"Do not worry," said his friend.

"I will help you get home."

"How?" asked Grandpa.

"I will shine my flashlight
across the river," he said.
"Then you can walk across
on the beam of light."

20

"No thanks!" said Grandpa.

"I know your tricks.

When I get halfway across,

you will turn the light off."

3. All of Our Noses Are Here

The Browns went for a ride

in their rowboat.

When the sun began to go down,

they rowed back to shore.

"Everyone line up,"

said Mr. Brown.

"Let us see

if anybody fell out of the boat.

One is here.

Two are here.

Three are here.

And four are here."

24

"But we are five,"

said Mrs. Brown.

"I think I counted wrong,"

said Mr. Brown.

"I will count again.

One is here.

Two are here.

Three are here.

And four are here."

"Only four?" asked Mrs. Brown.

"Yes," said Mr. Brown.

"One of us is missing."

Mrs. Brown began to cry.

So did the others.

"Why are all of you crying?"

a fisherman asked.

"Five of us went rowing,"

said Mr. Brown.

"But only four came back."

"Are you sure?"

the fisherman asked.

Mr. Brown counted again.

Again he counted only four.

"I know what is wrong,"

said the fisherman.

"You forgot to count yourself."

"I will try again,"

said Mr. Brown.

"One is here.

Two are here.

Three are here.

And four are here.

And *five* are here.

And SIX are here!"

"But there should be five,"
said Mrs. Brown.

"No," said Mr. Brown.

"Now we are six."

"But I do not see anybody else,"
said Mrs. Brown.

They looked in the rowboat

and under the dock

and up in the trees

and behind all the bushes,

but they did not find anyone.

"Come out! Come out!

Whoever you are!"

Mr. Brown shouted.

The others joined in,

but nobody came out.

When the fisherman

heard the shouting,

he went to see what was wrong.

"Now there are six of us

instead of five,"

said Mr. Brown.

"But we cannot find

this extra person."

"Are you sure there are six?"

the fisherman asked.

Mr. Brown counted again,

and again he counted six.

"You are doing it all wrong,"

said the fisherman.

"You counted yourself twice.

Let me show you

the right way to count.

Everybody, get down
on your hands and knees.
Now stick your noses
into the mud
and pull them out.

Now count the holes

your noses made."

Mr. Brown counted.

"One is here.

Two are here.

Three are here.

Four are here.

And *five* are here.

All of our noses are here!"

he said.

"Now we can go home."

4. The Best Boy in the World

There was no more wood

for the fire.

So Sam took his father's saw

and went to cut some wood.

He saw a dead branch

way up in an oak tree.

"That branch is just what I need,"

Sam said to himself.

Sam climbed the tree

and sat on the branch.

Then he began to cut it off.

Mrs. Brown was on her way to town

when she saw Sam

up in the tree.

"Sam!" she called.

"Get down from there!"

"Why?" he called back.

"If you cut off that branch,

it will fall,"

she said.

"And you will fall

and kill yourself.

That is why.

I am late for the beauty parlor.

So do what I say."

But when his mother left,

Sam started sawing again.

"What does my mother know

about cutting wood?"

he said to himself.

44

Suddenly Sam heard a *CRACK!*

The branch snapped off the tree,

and Sam tumbled down after it.

As he lay on the ground,

he thought,

"My mother said

this branch would fall,

and it fell.

And she said I would fall,

and I fell.

My mother is very smart.

She also said

I would kill myself.

So I must be dead."

Sam closed his eyes.

One hour later two old men

came out of the woods.

One of them was Grandpa.

"Look!" said Grandpa.

"It is Sam!

I wonder what is wrong."

"It looks as if he is dead,"
said his friend.
"Then we had better
carry him home,"
said Grandpa.

Soon they came

to a fork in the road.

"We go to the left," said Grandpa.

"No, we go to the right,"

said his friend.

They argued and argued,

but they could not agree.

Suddenly Sam spoke up.

"Excuse me," he said.

"When I was alive,

I always went to the left."

"You see," said Grandpa.

"I was right."

So left

was the way they went.

When they got home,

they put Sam down on the grass.

When Mrs. Brown got back

from the beauty parlor,

they told her

how they had found Sam.

53

"Are you sure he is dead?"

she asked.

"His eyes are closed,"

said Grandpa.

"He was a good boy,"

Grandpa's friend said.

"Good?" said Grandpa.

"He was the best boy in the world!

The finest!

The most terrific!"

When Sam heard that,

he opened his eyes.

"Sam!" cried Mrs. Brown.

"You are not dead anymore!"

"That is good," said Sam.

"When I was dead,

I missed my lunch.

And now I am starving.

Is there anything to eat?"

5. Sam's Girl Friend

Sam found a mirror.

It was the first mirror

he had ever seen.

When he looked in the mirror,

he saw his own face.

But Sam thought he was looking

at a picture of a boy

he did not know.

It was a magic picture.

Each time Sam made a face,

this boy made a face

back at him.

Sam showed the mirror to Jane.

She had never seen

a mirror before either.

"Look at the picture

of this boy," he said.

But when Jane looked in the mirror,

she saw a picture of a girl.

"This is not a picture of a boy,"

she said.

"It is a picture of a girl.

I bet she is your girl friend."

Sam's face turned red.

"Cut it out!" he said.

"I do not have a girl friend.

I do not even like girls."

"Yes, you do," said Jane.

"And you love this one a lot.

Everybody, look!

Here is a picture

of Sam's girl friend!"

Everyone looked in the mirror

at the same time.

"This must be a picture

of her whole family,"

said Mrs. Brown.

"They look very nice.

I will invite them all

to dinner."

Where the Stories Come from

"Jane Gets a Donkey" is based on one tale
in *Joe Miller's Jests* (1739) and on another from
the three hundred and eighty-eighth night of
the *Thousand and One Nights.*

"Grandpa Misses the Boat" is from an American
"Little Moron" story of the 1940s.

"All of Our Noses Are Here" is retold from
tales known in the southern United States and other
countries.

"The Best Boy in the World" is based on
a noodle story from India.

"Sam's Girl Friend" is based in part on
tales from southwestern United States and Japan
and Korea.

DATE DUE			
1/22/99 New			

C'

E
S

Schwartz, Alvin.

All of our noses are here, and other noodle tales.